Falco Tarassaco

AMSCUSAT

DAMANHUR

AMSCUSAT

by Falco Tarassaco

ISBN: 978-88-99652-13-5

Ist English edition (Ist Italian edition *Edizioni Horus 1980*)

Devodama srl, Vidracco (To) Italy
COPYRIGHT 2016© by DEVODAMA

Printed in June 2016

Thanks to Esperide Ananas for the translation and to Cinzia di Felice for the illustration on the cover.

CONTENTS

PREFACE

O n a planet entirely different from our Earth, in an undefined and exceptional time, the young Amscusat's life has constant surprises and emotions in store for us.

A highly advanced technology at the service of humanity and all living species, endowed with intelligence–this is the background to life on a planet in perfect balance, connected by synchronic lines to millions of other galaxies. The synchronic lines are stellar roads with enormous opportunities for trade, they open up fascinating scenarios of connection across space and time, enabling the material and spiritual growth of beings who share the desire for evolution. However, in the background to this world full of harmony and the highest quality of life, there looms a merciless war. Underway since time immemorial, this war ultimately proves far from over, perhaps owing to over confidence or an excess of pity on the part of the humans. From this point of view, this story carries a very clear warning.

The Enemy, the principle which materially opposes the evolution of intelligent species, ceaselessly pursues the inexorable destruction of all planets that seek

5

to oppose its advance, taking advantage of every opportunity that, voluntarily or otherwise, is afforded it. While epic and bloody clashes engulf distant galaxies, Amscusat meets fishes of various types, setjmeloolamj, setjvallà and many others, while in the sky shine moons and suns whose names derive from an ancient sacred language. On his planet every name has a meaning and the experiences lived increase the awareness of one's own nature and the absolute importance of the bonds between living beings in a free world. Here everyone is aware of the indisputable need for complex connections. This complete cross-over between species allows relationships among all living beings and with self–souls occupying metal bodies while awaiting a new incarnation. The almost total use of such advanced technology needs to be accompanied by the awareness of how, in other currents of time, many races still live cruel episodes of reciprocal subjugation; similarly, in the era of Amscusat, everyone has a clear sense of an evolutionary progression combined with ethical and moral values shared by all. Each species takes part in the experiences of others without the risk of ever losing its distinctiveness. Amscusat's days are spent between school lessons, visits to locations to improve his knowledge, a family made up of parents, co-parents, a myriad of natural and acquired relatives, and short journeys on which he often meets his contemporaries, including a dolphin who has always been his closest friend. So is this an *idyllic world where perfection can be said to have been attained once and for all?*

The common dream is to create a "paradise" happy and unique for everyone, characterized by an indissoluble link between awareness and knowledge. The out-of-the-body experience is used to visit the very well-stocked libraries on magic, and among sports activities gravisoccer (reminiscent of the Damanhurian tricalcio of our age) is very popular, and then there is metratura (another Damanhurian discipline) considered a sport-meditation technique of the highest level.

Immediate reincarnation is reserved for individuals with a developed consciousness and is very important in maturing and stratifying individual skills, at least those considered vital to good progress in the fight against the Enemy.

The anti-life principle is always in the thoughts of the young Amscusat, well aware that the future of the species which have chosen to counteract the Enemy's expansion–even at the risk of their very existence–depends on the outcome of a limitless war.

The lives of the allied races inhabiting billions of planets continue to be in danger without a final victory in sight against this ruthless and powerful force.

Everyone knows that the Enemy is fighting those who attempt to fight it, because it does not want to leave the slightest room for those who want to progress in their evolution.

This is a war that is relentless, a fight with no holds barred, in which the allied species have achieved substantial successes, managing to liberate planets that would otherwise be destroyed.

These peoples share an infinite wealth of knowledge, aware of the existence and the agreement with divinities who act in perfect harmony with living species to counter the Enemy.

In this, as in other moments of time, the Enemy acts by entering in every living being in order to undermine the progress of the species from a physical, spiritual, ecological and environmental standpoint.

But in what time, in what historical period, is this story set?

This is a war that has lasted millennia, during which countless species with free will come and go, the protagonists of a battle that seems to have no end and that seems set in a far distant future.

What if, instead, the adventures of the young Amscusat were only the fascinating memory of a struggle that in some way has already taken place somewhere in the folds of time, one in which the Enemy was able to insinuate itself in among species, to divide them, putting in question for the enth time the evolutionary advances achieved?

Of course, this could be the brief chronicle of a period of respite between wars conducted by a galactic empire where the ever-present technology ensures the attaining of all objectives, yet without saving humanity from the gravest of errors, which will negate all the successes achieved until then. In other myths, too, there are stories told of civilizations enjoying refined material and spiritual evolution being wiped out by mistaken interpretations leading to disastrous involution.

So, is this the end of an unknown branch of history or the beginning of renewed, striving awareness? In the relentless, but not infinite cycle of reincarnation there are Masters who go back into the game, willing to give their own lives in facing painful but necessary trials to restore hope to those who will not bend before the principle of anti-life.

Journeys of the soul, exchange of experiences and highly advanced technologies characterize, to some extent, all known times and galaxies, yet imagination and creative thinking will always prove powerful weapons to stimulate ever more discoveries, because often the best ideas come from individuals capable of a small, brilliant stroke of genius.

As Falco Terrassaco put it in one of his Thursday evening meetings with visitors and citizens in Damanhur, "we still sometimes have a banal idea of the universe, of life, of complexity, of space-time across the dimensions. When we think of complexity we almost always imagine spaceships and complex devices, but in the universe that can be considered truly evolved there are no more spaceships, since such things are used only at the dawn of any galactic civilization.

Rather, we could imagine an entire galaxy as if it were an immense city inhabited by several hundred million billion intelligent beings. Ultimately, the synchronic lines connect all points where there is life and they are nourished by that life growth exactly like the synapses of our brains. In fact, synapses that are most used strengthen the connections between specific neurons. So imagine it as follows: when you move in space-time it is better to use existing bodies in the worlds of arrival, ready and suited to those living conditions. Basically, in the universes travelling is easier as souls than in the body, and it is much more convenient to transfer information and knowledge rather than objects, to then build the latter with the raw materials of the planet of destination. When we talk about science-fiction, universes, technologies, we need to think of something that–being truly complex–has no need of spaceships. At a very evolved level there are passages, portals, several other systems and billions of dimensions that can be used in endless ways. Let us remember that when we refer to a possible universe we are not even talking about a billionth of what exists, if not even smaller, and which in fact is smaller than a grain of sand compared to the entire solar system."

So why the story of adolescent Amscusat?

"We, today, in our world–observed Falco–are as if on a desert island, a planet of the fourth order that could be compared to a cosmic dump. From the point of view of feasible technologies Amscusat could even be considered an old story. Think about it: if there were no science fiction, or at least the ability to fantasize,

human beings would not know how to invent anything new. Every single line of this story can be used, as it is a concentration of many elements, some of them demonstrably fascinating and curious. I am convinced that the influence of science fiction on technology is useful indeed. I still cherish the hope that one day someone will write a book on science fiction seen as a stimulus that can broaden the cultural capacity of individuals."

In each one of us there is something of Amscusat, especially when the desire for redemption and fantasy become real creative sparks that fire our synapses, if only with a tiny snap.

Somewhere, in infinite space-time, we too can find the Arielvo spaceship, forever concealed from the searching gaze of the Enemy, ready to do its part in enabling intelligent species to once more use guided incarnations.

In formulas and ritual oaths there is the anti virus that helps fight that which opposes spiritual and material union and evolution.

Coboldo Melo

AMSCUSAT

AMSCUSAT LOVED TO WALK ALONG THE HORIZON OF THE WARM SEA

A mscusat loved to walk, wearing his old monopole under-shoes as his grandfather used to, along the horizon of the warm sea. You know what that's like: a long slide as if cross-country skiing, your upper torso leaning forward, your hands behind the back like in skating, your thoughts lost in contemplation of the halting waves.

There were always curious fish following him, setjmeloolamj, setjvallà, thousands of other types, even a school of setjturà. Ecatfo shimmered pale in the sky, half as big as Alecat. He had not been on Ecatfo yet, as many of his friends had. Netila, for example, in firstlife, went with her mother to the lighted volcano Memen, inside its first chamber: an impressive spectacle, his friend said. Even now she speaks about it often.

And here she goes now, this is her typical call on the dental telephone: that tingle could only be her. He should not have given her his personal access code, she called him way too often. Luckily, in thirdlife the codes all change, otherwise all those not-chosen childhood friends could become a real nuisance.

"Just a couple of words Amscusat, as you have not yet arrived, remember that by today we must decide about your personal self-determined study-program. If you want to join us, we'll all meet later, at secondsun."

Meanwhile, Lavallaorò draws white stripes in the sky, small and frantic as always; while Oromè climbs, slow and serious, in the direction of midday. Four passages of the small sun during the day, four at night. What a bore this planet is. There are many which are much more vital, his friends say.

Amscusat is bored, he does not feel like joining his friends. He would take kicks at the fishes, if he could, and were it not an immoral action.

16

Amscusat chose his name according to tradition. Only in thirdlife will he be allowed to change or to confirm it. His pre-birth memories, under re-construction, led him to trips that so far were not too interesting. But his parents and god-parents always willingly accompanied him.

They say that somebody, once, invented a life for himself, because he wanted to see Alfocal, firstworld. He went there accompanied, according to tradition, at the expense of the universal memory fund. And just when he thought he had done something really cool, deceiving everybody, they left him there, where he still lives, all through his secondlife, according to the punishment decreed by the regional Alebal.

NECATOA, A METHANE-
BREATHING TUJLNE

A mscusat feels a strong attraction for Gedjfocal, the heavy world of the Caotat system. He said so to his Soul Guide, and since then his dreams have become more colorful: you can see that clearly in the many recordings in his diary. From time to time he chooses the second-level interpretation program, the one usually reserved to the more mature secondlifer. But nobody scolds him for this.

Amscusat is proud of his dream diary; so far he has made good exchanges with his friends, and with a boy from another system, Necatoa, who is really fun, even though there are some communication difficulties, as he is a methane-breathing Tujlne. Everybody today, in their first and second life, has an alien correspondent and they must learn the reciprocal system of communication. It is a part of the school program.

Following the Synchronic Lines–the lines of energy that link all the planets in the universe–of his current birth-world through his maturity code, Amscusat tried to trace his life-line from Algea, the firstworld of the firstsystem.

This is something that all youngsters try to do. Co-parents all smile, and each of them says how they tried, at least ten times, at their age. Very few succeed in doing it at such an early age, and some people don't ever manage to do it. So they resort to the Alebal, or even the Alalebal.

Amscusat has already learnt how to talk with two of himself, and he's proud of that, because this is an important step in his growth, just like learning to walk at an early age, or being able to ride the gravicycle without lateral supports. But today nothing seems to be working for him. Boredom, boredom, boredom.

And when he thinks of it, it does bother him a bit that he is not as good as his friend Netila in communicating with "selfs," the intelligences that inhabit metals, or with the super-lifes, the souls that are transitioning while waiting for a suitable body, as they wander on the Synchronic Lines among worlds, according to their program.

18

UNDERWATER INSIDE THE ENERGY BUBBLE

UNDERWATER INSIDE
THE ENERGY BUBBLE

Maybe it is time to go back. The sea is swelling and the clouds, looking like long stripes of light because of Lavallaorò, are getting denser and denser. It will rain. There will be a storm and sometimes during these tempests the horizonter doesn't work very well. At a brisk pace, he will be at home by focaor, when firstsun will start going down from its zenith.

The waves are getting more violent, just beyond his magnetic densosphere, so much so that they submerge it for long moments. It is probably better to lower the sound a bit, because it is getting frightening. There is wind, out there, whistling, and the water foams on the swollen waves.

How did people get around, when the energy bubbles did not exist? He actually knows it very well, he knows everything about boats and ships. He even went on board once. How amusing that was! Yet, it seems absurd to him that such primitive technologies could be really used to travel...

And what if its bubble let the energy out, if his small, minuscule, invisible, little island were not strong enough, here on the surface, and if he got wet and had to swim, in danger, suffocated by the water... but these are just figments of his imagination, fears emerging - as is the case - from a far away life. They always give him a shiver. Ancestral memories rightly stir us, reminding those of us who forget our origins, that we always are just fragile humans.

Anyway, it is better to go underwater. Inside his bubble Amscusat goes down towards the bottom, under the surface of the waters. Going all the way down to the abyss would be too much, because it would then be necessary to walk-slip for a much longer route back than the one he took to get here.

Underwater there is a completely different world.

There are the lights of the sea farms, dolphins selling tamed fish, large geothermal power stations, remnants of an ancient past that are no more in use and have been turned into a national monument. At a distance Amscusat also sees the underwater mines for the neutropower stations where all the substances and the metals necessary for home industries are made atom after atom, at different pressures.

Down here is also the great marine park of the warm river, the stream that crosses half the planet all the way up, almost to the thousand cold islands. Once he went there with his co-mother, for the usual medical examinations inside the genetic cabin, the de-composers of atoms. Because of how they work, many people jokingly call them "whisks."

20

It is very easy: you enter the cabin, the machine and a psychoanalyzer examine the organism, molecule after molecule, and they compare the parental genetic map and the individual chart with the reality of the body. If something is not right, all it takes is a short transfer from the "whisk" to a nearby cabin.

All the faulty or sick parts remain inside the "whisk" and they are re-densified and re-constructed with new material in the second cabin.

In a few minutes the analysis is over, and so is the cure and you are new! The treatment is completed by a "freshening up" of the vital aura, then the experts give you some warnings and suggestions on how to use proper dreams for healing, and off you go. They are all amicable and happy people, our health practitioners.

Whisk-cabins are used for many other functions, also to move from one place to the next. How much he would like to have one of them nearby right now. His co-grandfather Mabeimen–who is probably his favorite relative–does not like to use these whisks.

He often says that these small trips are useless, it is better to communicate directly with laservideodensity apparitions, but firstfather says it is not very kind to do so. Mama never speaks of these things, she shakes her head and says that they just try to get on each other's nerves; they never got along and they never will, not even in ninthlife.

MOLECULAR
MICRO-MACHINES
TO BUILD SAND CASTLES

Amscusat continues to glide fast underwater. Cold islands, warm streams, vague and bored thoughts, images of his parents, his friends, things of everyday life pass sideways across Amscusat's mind, while he has to pay closer attention finding his way home, now that he is under the surface.

If he turns up the volume inside his bubble, he can hear the uproar of the great sea, above him and under him. He's a little apprehensive. Better to call home through the dental code and ask for an orientation signal. He must swallow his pride a little, in these cases. It is better to get a frown from his mother, than making her worry for fear of interfering.

The balance of the bubble is not great, a constant wavelike movement upsets Amscusat's inner ear, and his stomach churns. Maybe it is better to continue his walk on the surface.

Amscusat goes up. All around him is a pandemonium. It's becoming harder and harder to walk-skate towards the solid ground.

He is almost there: after passing by the rocks, even if it rains, he will be able to turn the shoe monopole off and go up to the nearest cabin-station. And then he can finally reach home, sixty miles away, and maybe there is no rain scheduled for that area now.

The internal computer-adviser is giving him advice and that bores him. Amscusat has heard all those warnings a thousand times before. Nevertheless, even though he does not want to admit it, that little voice has been a constant friend, ever since his firstlife phases. It was a present of his maternal co-parents.

His older genetic brother, on the other hand, gave him a ring with six micro-construction-machines set in it. They are the small molecular type, the ones that you can direct when you learn to control your dental code and your finger movements. Ideal micro-machines for building sand castles, grain after grain, making them adhere to each other with the right program.

He had always been fascinated by those minuscule insect-devices. He loves maneuvering them at close hand, creating fancy castles, towers, suspension bridges and statues. His are just children's games, but this technology is used also for many very important functions.

Also inside him there are micro molecular-medical-machines which, using the same system, can quickly repair any damage to his body. Everybody receives subcutaneous injections to insert the nano-machines, and they all know they have these specialized devices inside. Everybody studies this, in every school of the world.

THE GREAT VITAL
REVOLUTION

A mscusat loves animals. A second-classification dog lived with him, one of those who have the right to vote for all matters concerning their species, according to the Conventional Treaty among symbiotic living forms.

His human and mechanical teachers told him that there was a time in which animals were considered inferior to human beings, unable to think and make decisions independently. At that time, very few knew how to communicate between species, and humans considered themselves a species per se, as if they did not belong to the same vital line.

There are many species outside the Treaty and there are food-bodies, but today nobody is surprised nor complains about it. The agreement among species, the food supplying-exchange is part of nature, a balance to be respected without excesses, stable in number.

Sentient souls move. The body is eaten, and they choose a different and higher experience level, as soon as they are mature. All species agree on these points. The times of prevarication are over.

Group-races can only be tamed, and used for shared food, in great variety. And people can also choose to eat meat that has been grown in a lab, just from a few cells of the living animal. There are indeed many kinds of lab-grown meat, including human meat that apparently has a pleasant taste, even though Amscusat is a bit horrified by it... young people his age find it trendy to eat the grown meat of reptiles.

Once, violence created the same balance, but without being aware. With the Treaty, the bridge-species to which Amscusat belongs, started the great vital revolution, bringing balance among a very great variety of forms. After all, this is one of the tasks of a bridge species, a species that knows it has a physical and a divine part, and it is a means of connection between the material plane and the spiritual and divine ones.

Today, everybody on this world considers the species and the vital transformations as adaptations with the same value, none superior nor inferior, but with only temporarily major or minor roles to play.

They say that, on the minor worlds, there are people so parochial and narrow-minded they cannot accept, in case of transfer for an activity, changing their body and taking one more suitable for the environment.

Can this be possible? Can this be true? Amscusat, like everybody else, has tried new bodies, mechanical or cellular transfers, as part of his school training.

There are fashionable bodies, which one of his co-mothers often changes, out of pleasure, just for fun.

Once he met her and he did not even recognize her. She had a great time making fun of him, before he realized it was her. Grandfather Mabeimen does not approve of these things.

He considers them excessive, but it is logical, when you don't change bodies in a long time, as he did, then you may end up thinking like this. Amscusat knows that his grandfather, even when he changes, always prefers to choose older bodies. All tastes are tastes. Maybe, one day, he'll also prefer not to change too much down the age range. Also a certain fashion says to do so, after all.

Tonight, after Oromè's sunset, Amscusat will go with his firstdad to a concert of birds, conducted by a famous flyer. Those species have been able to translate their music for humans, and today it is much in demand.

27

He also liked very much the dance of the abyss octopuses he saw nine suns ago, with an accompaniment by whales. At live human concerts, he often sees that the basins for sea creatures are full. Dolphins and orcas like certain shows very much, including the dance ones; for them it's always very funny to watch the movements of the land species.

THE GRAVICYCLE

But now, he has to get back home. Amscusat calls firstmother. She's not in. The home computer answers. Amscusat asks it to send him his gravicycle, for he wants to get back by road instead of via cabin. Within a few minutes, from the closest station, his cross-country vehicle appears, diligently teletransported.

It is still raining, but a little rain is surely not bad for a healthy body like his. He hooks his monopole under-shoes to the seat and then he gets on his cycle. Noiselessly, the gravicycle lifts up, above the grass lawn that is soaking wet with lukewarm water.

How beautiful and amusing it is to pedal. If he does it really hard he can sometimes rise up to two meters. Now, he is just a few centimeters above the surface, Sixty miles is not a great distance, but proportion requires the right means, as his bone-computer often says.

In order to navigate among the stars, gravity ships are needed, those that carry with them a black hole, right for that purpose.

For journeys among systems of the same area, it is enough to use extra-dimensional vessels, those able to shorten distances by going through the most suitable dimensions.

29

Within the same solar system, transmission cabins are normally used, that are special super calibrated whiskers.

Magnetic-levitating mini ships are also used and, for sports lovers, also nuclear plasma shuttles. In a prehistoric representation, he even saw some chemical rockets being used!

There are also exploration stations, used to contact the species of different worlds that are really far away. Infra-galactic and super-insular galactic. Wow, those are real spaceships!

His paternal grandfather, Aminepetaà, was crazy about traveling and, even now, likes continuing in that job. He enters a tele-transference cabin, reaches several intermediate stations on spaceships and spends many suns tracing vital synchronic lines, in their strangest ramifications.

In his long life in his present average form, he met four new living human species of bridge-human form level and hundreds of non-bridge sub-human species. And he even took part in drafting interlife treaties with some of them. He has always been very active. Maybe one day, also he, Amscusat, will enjoy to do similar things.

Now he does not know what he wants, he is bored, maybe a little less than before, but he pedals slowly and idly. What a day! Ecatfo has set, and so has Lavallaorò. There are fewer shadows, the colors are paler, even though Oromè, beyond the clouds, shows its presence. Anyhow, the rain is already stopping and the clouds are fraying.

Next time he will ask his internal computer to inform him when it is about to rain. He hardly has the time to think of this that his bracelet diligently tells him that it had warned him, even before he put on his monopole under-shoes, before strolling on the water.

But Amscusat had obliged it to keep silent. A typical computer reaction, just as Amscusat's is typical of a firstlifer, and also of a secondlifer. Adults use many words, such as emotional disorders or pubertal stimuli to define Amscusat's mood.

He shrugs, but a little smile spreads over his face. He pedals faster, rising up high on his gravicycle. Just as the clouds are dissolving, so is his gloomy boyish mood. In the far distance he sees two other young people on their gravicycles.

"Let's reach them," he says to himself. They wait for him. One is a boy he has already met, the other one is a girl he has never seen before, she looks friendly and eager to chat.

31

WRIST SPHEROSELF FOR GORILLAS

H er name is Netra, she lives in nearby tree-house, and he gladly accepts her invitation for an ice-cream at her place. Tree-houses are plant buildings, acquired thanks to a treaty with the world of plants.

The shape of the trunks, the branches and the leaves are modified in order to create rooms, stairs, little halls and terraces.

Everything is very personalized. Solar, geothermic or nuclear accumulators create the right temperature for every room. It is a beautiful house, spacious, airy and nicely fragranced.

Netra, while her friends make themselves at home, changes her alive-robe for a mantle-animal in another color. The creature is very happy when its owner wears it, and it greets her joyfully.

This species does not have an inter-species treaty as yet, as it is too simple. Netra shows her friends her favorite musical instrument and entertains them, playing: it is a tensochord with variable sound box, from which she obtains very enjoyable sound-emotional tunes. His boredom has evaporated, like the clouds in the sky.

33

Meanwhile the other boy, a thirdlifer, talks about the war front, down there in the nebulas, where the clash with the Enemy is now direct. There are great ships with neutron armors, the joy-throwers, the active sun-extinguisher, the anti-life sowers and the psycho-projectors of the allies.

Napna, for that's his name, talks about his gorilla mate he met down there only twenty suns ago. He seems enthusiastic about this very evolved allied race, describing their wrist-spheroselfs, that send emotional states against the Enemy.

He says that this is, indeed, one of the most effective weapons against the Isajtà. He even shows a projection of his alien friend, Enchidu, by means of his pocket densifying-projector.

In turn, Amscusat talks about the courses in natural levitation he's attending and the specialization in natural telekinesis he wants to learn. He is happy to have something exciting to tell about himself, too. After all, the afternoon didn't turned out to be as boring as at first it had seemed.

Netra is interesting, but the time to get back home is getting closer and closer. Amscusat gets on the seat of his gravicycle, says goodbye to everybody and off he goes, passionately pedaling his way home. Only twenty more miles to go. The countryside around him is wonderful, free, rich in life and full of light.

Nowadays, on advanced planets, all industrial activities are carried out hundreds of meters underground, way beneath the water-table so there is no risk of pollution, and the surface is not disfigured. Sharing of the land is a common asset and also the non-human species have rights that must be respected.

Along the way, a raccoon calls him on the inter-species emergency communication system: it needs help because one of its pups has almost drowned in the rainstorm.

The intervention, thanks to the portable doctor featured in the gravicycle, is fast and in time: a good dose of artificial breathing and a few pranatherapy passages–which Amscusat learned during the second level of the Course on Animal Lives–quickly produce the wanted result.

From time to time, Amscusat wonders how it is possible that a species as intelligent as this one constantly prefers to have no intervention or interference from technologies different from those they can develop with their natural limbs.

35

But this concerns ways of thinking, and the point of view of races and species that have made their own choice. This must be respected, not judged.

CONCERT OF THE COLLECTIVE OF FLYING SPECIES

A mscusat arrives home. As he enters, he discovers that there is mail for him. It is a psychometric object, sent by a far-away friend. It came via ordinary post - and therefore rather extraordinary in these times - not through the usual whisk transmission.

If sent via a normal cabin, psycho-charged objects cannot retain psychometric and emotional characteristics, while a postal sending, of course, does not affect the object and the emotional signals it contains.

Dad arrives home, too. In a little while, they'll go together to see a concert offered by a collective of flying species, in the Art City. For that kind of distance, they would take the underground pneumatic train, whose taxi-stations are located under every house, almost everywhere. Descensor to the second level, under the stores, and off they go.

Once on the train, Amscusat realized he is still a bit hungry, even if he had already had dinner once. He chooses a self-heating sea food from the carriage buffet. It is a variety of algae and cereal pasta.

Amscusat and his father are now under the city, the elevator takes them straight down inside the hall of the multiracial concert, where dolphins, whales, and various primates, dogs, horses, meerkats, lions and dozens of other species are already waiting for the concert to start, each one of them in their specific sectors. There are many exchanges of greetings, olfactory signals translated into many different languages.

In the sector reserved to visitors from other worlds, Amscusat sees a Necatbet for the first time. The being has vegetable hair and five heads talking one to the other. This is a race famous for its mathematical abilities, and olfactory-visual papers very often talk about them.

38

The Necatbet is located in a special container, where pressure is about fifty atmospheres, and he breathes a mixture of impoverished oxygen and other rather flammable gases.

Dad tells Amscusat that mother Mana has received the agreement for another child. A baby girl whose re-called soul would be that of a very good composer. Amscusat is happy about this programmed birth. So, he will become an elder brother, at last!

His own older genetic brother, Ilna, very rarely spends any time with Amscusat. He is interested only in the competitions of light.

He says he is an artist composing the rustling of the trees, and this is all he talks about, at the moment. He seeks Consciousness, as everyone feels they need to do, as the mission of each interlife.

In the concert hall, the lights, and the different emitters of light frequencies appropriate for each of the species, get softer. All the audience prepare for the common prayer, before watching the concert.

Everybody, each in their own specific way, makes contact with the Divine Forces, by intercession of the Universal Sacred Fire. The minds of so many different races concentrate with fervor, on the flame, Fatbaet, the living fire that collects the differences and re-unites them in God. Re-unites them in different names and comprehension, even in the religions of the more backward species, because they too are worthy or respect.

Once everyone is singing, whistling, scenting, smelling, yelling and ritual movements are over, the famous bird Oolamilla gets ready to conduct the concert. There are one thousand seven hundred flying singers, representing two hundred and sixteen species. Soloists, choirs, duets, quintets, execute the harmonic ensemble with great ability and with their typical, splendid sense of rhythm.

For the occasion, many trees have agreed to be transferred onto the scene, and they themselves are an integrated part of the opera, through sound translators, which present to the public the tree version of the concert.

For the species that have no sense of hearing, there are the usual translation facilities, bringing the work to the comprehension of any human, animal, or alien race.

Inside their cabins, perfumes are produced, as well as impossible sounds, vibrations and colors, that for us humans would have no meaning, but they do for other beings.

Amscusat is enthusiastic about the concert. Never before had he been at such a complex work. He looks forward to the moment in which he will tell his friends about this, even though no words will be able to convey all the emotions, sensations and feelings the opera transmitted to him...

For this reason, he records everything in Emo-program mode, so his friends will be able to share the state of mind he was in during the concert.

When the concert is over, after the ritual acknowledgments and appreciations of everyone, the artists as well as the audience, it is time to return home.

MOTHER MANA AND FIRSTDAD CODAJI

O n the way back, on the level of the shopping mall, father Codaji buys a couple of dream-tapes for himself and for Amscusat. They are new compilations, the dreams of many different races, some of them aliens, not yet in contact with the Galactic Civilization. Firstdad is an archaeologist.

He always looks for inspiration for his researches in these recordings. To Amscusat, they are just strange adventures that take him out of his usual life.

Back at home, Codaji and Amscusat greet mom and celebrate the future programmed child. Ilna is also there, talking enthusiastically about the concert, which he attended from the out-of-body circle, being not able to enter the theatre, due to the large crowd.

Of course, his brother's interest mostly concerns the interpretation of the trees. So a discussion starts, and each one of them shares their ideas with great passion. Mother Mana brings about peace among them, before their sharing becomes a heated argument.

They all drink a herb tea together and then it's time to go to sleep.

Everybody has a different kind of bed, according to personal taste. In secondlife, many normally prefer the living mats on the floor, but such inclinations change, with age. Ilna, for instance, loves de-gravitated beds, while Amscusat's parents have for years been using plant mattresses.

Father and mother have recently renewed their marriage, and Secondmother also desires to become a closer relative, by adopting both Ilna and Amscusat, if they would agree. Jpialra - this is her name - deals in dimensiobags, those which look like small flexible pockets, with the bottom out of focus.

You can put in and take out, objects up to the volume of one cubic meter and with indefinite weight. Nowadays, they are used mostly by explorers and by the military, who have problems of space and volume, and turn them into real wishing wells. Amscusat has one, too.

He uses it at school, when they go on excursions to the unexplored territories of animal species of the Interlife Treaty. It is so useful! He packs it with his pneumo-tent, food, objects for authorized exchanges, monopole under-shoes and other various tools.

Amscusat thinks of what he'll have to do tomorrow, when he goes with his class to the time labs, for the yearly aptitude tests. For his exam, he'll have to find out something more of the past lives of many historical figures. He will have to prove that he can follow a given signal, as a reference of a time period, and trace back the person he's looking for.

It is not one of the subjects that Amscusat prefers, even though, in its own way, it is always very intriguing. Isipeal, one of his co-parents and a friend of his mother's is involved in time travel. He gave Amscusat a few lessons on tracing, the method used to follow an individual's signal through the years.

But Amscusat finds it much more fun to follow events in other epochs using animals living in those times as exploration agents. He uses his senses, and the ability lies in being able to move from the eyesight of a bird to the hearing of a hare, from the sense of smell of a dog and then again to the eyesight of a cat, for instance... all in a flow.

In this way it is possible to observe important events and people, great discoveries and inventions with an effect similar to what several multi-sensory cameras would produce. Normally, these cameras are used to document galactic shows of national relevance.

Amscusat likes to carry out these exercises using the senses of the insects present at the various epochs... this is an inclination typical of his generation, just to be different from the older one.

Before going to sleep, Amscusat turns on the dream-tape...

43

THE MARKET OF DREAMS

G oodnight. Dreams are interesting. Living someone else's experiences enriches sympathy and tolerance, so, our parochial sense is attenuated a little, even if we live far away from the central worlds. This dream comes from far away, a barbaric world, where reality sometimes has aberrant aspects, where the Enemy still acts with full power.

There are unfamiliar scenes and adventures, unknown and intriguing objects, animals that have not reached the level of the Treaty and are sometimes used in a terrible way. Amscusat likes to think that he is a secret agent, on a mission against the Enemy of allied lives, that proteiform Enemy dividing the species, putting one against the other.

How varied is the universe! If there were no internal computers so many memories and experiences would be lost, instead of being kept in the added memory, so they can return to consciousness when necessary.

During sleep, the micro-machines work at their best and regeneration rays massage those muscles which have not been used much during the day, keeping them efficient and well trained. Nowadays, to sleep means to put experiences in order, to travel out-of-body, if you are an appointment with your friends, or if you're following a particular course out of the thousands offered especially for the night phases.

There are people who work directly on other people's dreams, selling all kinds of out-of-body courses, sometimes as their second job, especially students needing money. The market of dreams is one of the most flourishing activities, but also regeneration programs, seminars, guided journeys and night teaching of any specialization, all are very successful.

There are many subscribers to dream-transmissions, which offer continuous successful stories or special programs according to the client's tastes. In this period, for instance, the most popular broadcast is a serial of dream-visions on the great characters of Alefocal's deep seas.

There are also complete series, for collectors. Life scenes from barbarian planets or from others with very special peculiarities. Possible stories number billions and billions, suited to every species and every possible taste.

And, last but not least, there are also the divine channels, from which trans-bridge species train more backward ones, through Knowledge. So many, are those divine or para-divine categories, in harmony with the whole. Their power and wisdom can be compared to those of humankind today, in relation to minor species, not yet part of the Interlife Treaty.

There are also channels for sub-divine forms, sponsored by their prophets, who offer synchronic interventions in many specializations typical of human desires.

But they're all just remains of religious movements, about to disappear.

Of course you can, and you must, leave some time for total rest. You can choose when to sleep, according to the things you have to do, your will, your interests. Your body and the mind are regenerated, cleansed and rejuvenated, in every single cell which requires it.

EXAM TOPIC: TIME SPHERES

A fter his sleep, Amscusat is called on his dental line by his friend Netila, to make arrangements and go together to the place of the time examination. Amscusat is a bit nervous: it is not just a matter of remembering mnemonic data. Today, that problem does not exist. He will have to show that he has understood principles and procedures for interventions in the different disciplines. His computer-bracelet gives him its typical, rather pedantic, advice.

49

Anyway, it is still early. Amscusat has some time to eat something good, while Lavallaorò leaps in the sky, followed shortly after by the slower Oromè. There are both whole and refined foods, ideal for his developing body that is well prepared thanks to his strong and well nourished aura.

Fruit from the fresh region, insects cooked in thousands of tasty fashions, salads and vegetables, fish and supplements right for the mental and physical formation chosen at the time of the birth programming.

There is very little meat–and in any case, only the kinds grown in a lab, from cells of different organs–chestnuts, berries, and some delicacies consisting of bio-formed constructions, built by artist-technicians or imported from other fashionable worlds.

While his personal computer makes him go over all the lessons in time technique, Amscusat has time to play a little and relax, projecting his senses into an insect-micromachine and trying to cross the lawn in front of his house.

He is training for the pseudo-insect race he has challenged his friends to compete with him in. It is difficult. The dangers are thousands and all new, real and able to give him emotions, because of their violence. With grass as high as trees, other quite aggressive (real!) insects, extremely varied terrain, and many hungry birds nearby, even a journey of a few meters is dangerous and very exciting.

It is now time for Amscusat to go to his appointment and, unwillingly, he stops playing. He takes the underground train, and he arrives at his destination in very few minutes. Netila is already waiting for him; she behaves a little like an additional co-mother, even though they are the same age. She is excellent at atomic constructions.

One day, she will become a moulder of new substances or a psychic guide in the analysis of alien materials. She often talks about this, and with conviction. Amscusat doesn't know why, but when he listen to her, he often thinks of grandfather Mabeimen, and his old job as programmer of home robots. A strange mental link. Maybe it is because of all the funny episodes his grandfather Mabeimen told him over the years.

Like that time when, thinking he had to program some home robots with very complex behaviors, chosen by his clients, he did so in the wrong home.

Amscusat always laughs at the thought of how the robots' owners must have reacted, arriving back home and finding their robots behaving in a totally different way, not knowing why.

He goes with Netila into the training classroom, where there are several time spheres, ready for use. Everyone is given a specific examination task. He is to find traces and the works of a famous painter from the past, with very few starting indications.

From the time traces of one of the artist's paintings, Amscusat finds the period, and from the material the painter used in it, he localizes the place. After a few hours, he has finally found out who the person is, as well as some of the salient traits of his character and originality.

51

He carries out his task thoroughly and is able to find also some traces of the artist's following incarnations, up to the maximum point a stranger is allowed to investigate, according to the legal norms of behavior. It was not easy, but it would have been even more difficult to discover alien artists because works are based on different sense fruition. It becomes very complicated to imagine certain processes that, on the contrary, are natural and usual to those belonging to the same form. All in all, the exam did not go badly, even though many other students had finished their research much sooner. Netila went away with her girlfriends, leaving a greeting message for him.

HIS SOUL MASTER IS WAITING FOR HIM

O romè is high in the sky, and also the two main moons are visible, although pale, at the two extremities of the sky. Amscusat starts feeling bored, as he did yesterday. He does not exactly know what to do, whether to go back home or take a walk.

Maybe the best thing to do is to go visit his Soul Guide, to get insight and comfort for these rather obsessive moods that have been making him suffer lately. His guide lives in another area of the wood-garden. Maybe he'll take a flying bubble there. Bubbles are actually flat disks with one, two, three, five and ten standing places.

They have a little balustrade around them and an energy field all around. Some are for humans and others are used by many different living species. Amscusat chooses a three-seat bubble, the nearest one, and he finds himself sharing his road–which is actually a grass path–with a small dog, which is going to see its brothers in the same area.

A little conversation, in the dog's warm and affectionate way, makes his day happier. The translator works well and the exchange of chat is pleasant.

The boy talks of himself and the things he is interested in, while the dog, whose name is Fasetmoan, talks about its job as guardian to the protected under-races in the North, beyond Damjmel, on the islands.

The dog arrives at its destination. They say goodbye to each other and it disembarks. Amscusat has not far to go. He decides to walk the last mile and sends the gravitational bubble back to the station.

His Soul Master is waiting for him; actually he is already walking toward him on the path. It is reassuring and pleasant to meet him, even though, because of his shyness, Amscusat is always a bit scared before such meetings.

They talk, while walking together, about the anxieties of the young age, the world, the stars, and the living species including the newly discovered ones; of the war far away but not so distant; of the Enemy and themselves.

His Soul Master is a fourthlifer. He's been taking care of Amscusat for a long time, preparing him for his future choices, for at least two incarnations. Amscusat does not remember much of those lives, yet.

He only gets flashes that he can distinguish in his dreams, or in some moments set by his daily rhythm. The chat is pleasant and useful, the Master's advice valuable and his indications and suggestions well accepted.

More at peace with himself, Amscusat takes the underground train from the house of his Soul Master and goes to the city center, where some of the service buildings are on the surface and not underground. He calls a few friends, via dental phone, to find out where they are and arrange a meeting.

THE SPACESHIP ARIELVO

A s he thought, his friends are gathered at the place where he is going to, under the city tower. The big tower is almost one mile tall, soaring high, and at the summit, a large dish-terrace hosts a park for high altitude species and ornamental water features.

The usual meeting point of Amscusat and his friends is next to a vapor fountain, where energy fields create foggy and colorful sculptures that change constantly. The fountain silently tells the history of the city, with its most important characterizing events.

The group talks about all sorts of things. Time flies happily, with jokes and witty remarks. Besides the humans, there are also a young horse and a dog with a strange sense of humor. After a while Falna also arrives, an eagle who is part of the group.

Amscusat called Falna himself, by dental phone, during the ride on the underground train. Falna and the human boy are close friends. They often take each other's side, during the group discussions.

The eagle is a secondlifer. The horse Fadjfal is good at mathematics. The dog is a lover of botany. Each friend has a different hobby, but they all share an interest in the great star ships.

57

In the program that starts around the time of Caor, when Oromè goes down, a one-week visit to a great spaceship is scheduled. A week is the minimum time needed for a visit, although still a superficial one. The ship is moored in orbit, before leaving again for the far front. They have all been waiting for months for this occasion.

The ship Arielvo is a sphere with a diameter of twenty miles. It carries 60,000 minor fighter ships and about twenty million fighting robots. It is driven by eight hundred general minds in parallel, mostly of human beings, dolphins, elephants and killer whales.

The crew is composed of specialized representatives of at least two hundred extra planetary races, and there are sectors best suited to the gravities and the breathing gases of everyone. Normally, on these great ships, there are integrated species which are compatible under many aspects and have complementary lines of thought.

The ship is a world in miniature, including the sector of forests and lakes and other areas which reproduce the natural environments of almost all the hosted species, albeit on a small scale. There are factories capable of swallowing star dust, or wandering masses to turn them, atom by atom, into any programmed object, of whatever material it is made of.

Before each battle, the factories produce every possible kind of armament that seems useful, both assembled before or newly thought of. They swallow up whole moons and turn them into satellites, special substances, weapons or pure energy. And they do endless secret things.

58

In the programs of intervention, or colonization, these ships produce any object, any tool that can be useful on each specific planet. The biological crew is composed of a little more than two million beings.

In the divine contact sector, in the central Temple, a few protective divinities manifest themselves. They connect synchronic events to the lives of the whole crew, on every probable and magical plane. The main God of the ship is secret and hidden.

In this class, there are a few million ships, and they depend on the really huge ship carrying-stations. Such stations are normally created by hollowing a moon that is then lined with neutronium and other special states of energy-matter. Amscusat would love to visit a super-ship, but it takes almost one year just to explore one superficially.

ASSAMEN, THE WARRIOR-TREE

It is now time to say goodbye to parents and co-parents, and to the friend who will not take part in the visit to Arielvo. Those who are going are all very excited. They are about to reach the station, where the special whisk is located, which will transfer them to the great ship.

Unfortunately, the station is busy receiving and transferring the ship's crew, so the friends have no choice but to take a magnetic shuttle, and to reach Arielvo via orbit, instead of in that direct way. The inconvenience will make them lose some time.

But, anyway, in such matters, it is always better to adapt without complaining. The vehicle they reserve is an old fifty seater model, without pressurized sections for the gases that different species breath.

But it does not matter. A few marine people are also traveling with them. They sit in their water basins. It's easy to become friends; like going by bus to visit an ancient city, everybody is friendly and willing to help.

The shuttle lifts up from the small spaceport, in the big park, shaking softly the leaves of the trees.

There is also a big tree traveling with them, and they discover that it will be part of the crew. Through its modulators, the tree explains what its task will be, but it is difficult to grasp it fully.

It will be a sort of mental phone operator, to accelerate the subliminal connections of a part of the crew, in case of battle. The warrior-tree, called Assamen, is a veteran soldier, having fought many battles against the Enemy and its allies.

It knows how to relate its adventures with a warmth and emotion. As they get closer to the great war spaceship, the various species on the vehicle are all fascinated by these stories told by the big tree.

An interesting week lies ahead of Amscusat, with Assamen's war stories and the visit to the great ship. I, Amscusat's storytelling-diary, as my programmed time is over, leave my task to others.

THE STORYTELLING DIARY OF THE TREE ASSAMEN

I am the storytelling diary of the tree Assamen, officer of war communications on the ship Arielvo, at present in orbit around Alfocal. I am ready for recording.

Assamen is a few hundreds of years old. It is a fifthlifer from Algea, the first world. He took part in many battles in the last eighty years. It is during this time that the Enemy is being defeated in many systems. The war has taken a positive turn.

After thousands of years of desperate resistance, a few actions on planets that seemed of secondary importance–but which were strategically essential for the Synchronic Lines–have produced a general upheaval. The Enemy has been eradicated from many worlds. It was like a virus inside every inhabitant, save for a very few exceptions.

Many races have been freed. Some have been destroyed, because there was nothing left to be done. Their maximum time was over and they showed no sign of improvement. Unfortunately, in war, things like this may happen. Assamen perceives multifaceted light. Smell and other chemical signals are the senses it uses the most.

63

It has magnetic senses which enter other species, so it can perceive forms from the inside, as well as the outside. This natural habit allows it to examine events from points of view that no warm-blooded being can rival. Its species can correct micro-events around itself. This, for them, is the equivalent of their sense of touch, as if they had substitute arms and hands.

Assamen has learned how to move around inside a climate container for its roots, and a special suit creates and keeps the right atmosphere around it. Only its huge sensitivity to light creates some problems, because of the radiations of different suns: everybody knows that trees do not wear sunglasses.

From its assigned position, as tree officer of Space Navy, Assamen has seen the great Battle of Foursuns, when two spherical formations clashed, each composed of millions ships. It was a marginal, but legendary battle, largely because the minds of a few Enemy officers were penetrated by psycho-images that caused them to make serious mistakes in their maneuvers.

Before they could get back the reins of the situation, their formation was broken up and a few virus-ships had penetrated into the centre of their configuration. They had masked themselves as Enemy ships, and little by little, they managed to weaken some of the Enemy fleet's vital functions.

That time, the Enemy was not able to operate from the inside of the crew of many ships, because it had been discovered and eliminated.

The Enemy ships, in doubt because of the presence of our ships among theirs, in many cases started to fire on one another. They were desperately trying to identify, or were convinced of having found, the virus-ships.

Sterilizing suns and planets is a terrible thing, but sometimes it is necessary, sadly necessary. The common anti-life system of the Enemy consists of destroying vital planets, by causing irreparable ecological errors through well covered-up actions, but for the human federation this is intolerable.

However, in a couple of instances it was an inescapable choice. The high price was compensated by the destruction of individually identified Enemies, not only of their slaves and allied servants.

In star battles, at times there are also direct assaults of biological, mechanic and plasma-mechanic troops. Assamen has taken care of and co-ordinated some of these troops, just as in the famous battle which brought about the occupation and liberation of Focalce, a metallic planet, from which the Enemy fleets used to take off for their rampages and to disseminate their evil.

65

THE BATTLE OF FOCALCE

F rom over sixteen million battleships, there emerged small two-seater bio and mec assault craft. These specialized craft started to bore into the surface of the planet and they went down over four miles, burning and melting whatever they met on their way.

They found the large cave-factories and managed to block many of them, for the time needed to get the reinforcements there, and then dismantled them completely.

On the surface, and on the seas, the bio troops–many of whom were humans–made essential movements at subliminal velocity, driving with their servo-brain or intuitive sight, whenever they found themselves inside memory-canceling fields.

So, they managed to stand up to enormously strong armies, by bringing the battle on to their ground and by not getting confused, as the Enemies expected they would. On that occasions cannons shooting happiness and humor were used for the first time.

The dogs, with their sensitive hair-suits, and the flying explorers, conducted exemplary operations. Many infiltrations, by many allied races, managed to cause delays and unrepairable damages.

After a few hours, the situation was turning in our favor, while the reserve fleet was keeping the opponents' reinforcements under pressure at the system's borders.

Using degravitators and exploiting the direction of the light pressure, we managed to direct some very high plasma emissions from the surface of the suns: many Enemy ships were swallowed as they came towards us with suns behind them with the intention of dazzling us.

We managed to crash four moons onto the surface of Focalce, pushed there by neutron tow-ships, which were successfully materialized in a defined area inside the moons themselves.

It was the first time, maybe, that it was possible to project, via super-whisk, such a mass and then to direct it. None of the Enemy defenses had the time to divert the trajectory of the moons, which, without any serious damage, swept away the planetary defense shields by overcharging them and knocking them out.

For centuries and centuries the Enemy has used piloted blackholes and dimensional wells to swallow up millions of living worlds, whenever it realized that their living species had started to refuse it, to fight against it. But the secret worlds, for millennia, have eluded its search, just as the many agents who, in time, have been able to free other worlds, through new techniques.

We do not know if this synchronic phase will bring us victory, or if one day the Enemy, expelled from the central galaxies, will be able to come back and to nullify the living.

In the meantime, Assamen will always do what free will allows. It has reached enlightenment and fully understands its destiny. It is said that its species, when it reaches comprehension, knows what its death is going to be, and having assessed whether the life it leads is rich and worthy, accepts its fate without trying to modify it, acknowledging this as the cost.

Now let us return to Amscusat's story-telling diary. I, Assamen's narrating diary, have for the moment, concluded my task.

INSIDE ARIELVO'S ARMOR

A mscusat has arrived on the great ship Arielvo, for a quick visit, which will last just one week. The spaceship has a layer of external armor, made of metallic diamond, built by special micro-machines and involving decades of work. Between the first and the second layer, there are special gases able to re-condense possible damage and to re-build the outside shield, with the help of billions of other micro-machines.

71

The third layer is super-magnetic plasma-material, a state of matter in which energy and mass are in constant inverse proportion. It contains a mixture of fluctuating atoms in creative formation, so that the matter thus formed is not stable, never remaining the same for more than a few millionth of a second. Underneath, there are layers of absolute void, and of alternated super flexible metals, such as iron, lead, copper, gold, silica, metallic water and condensed ultra-lightweight gases.

Each layer has a thickness of a minimum of two meters, and a maximum of seventy. A living nervation of mnemonic metals keeps all the structure in reactive tension, to compensate for all the stresses the great machine is submitted to. Synchroactive pluridimensional strata complete the external shield.

In orbit around the spaceship, at a distance of about a hundred miles, gravitate twenty-four satellites, at very high speed and perfectly synchronized. They form a hyper-nuclear intercepting barrier, capable of stopping almost all known weapons.

A magnetic and bi-dimensional or seven-dimensional energy superfield extends even farther; it can deviate and modify the state of being of any substance composed of atoms or antimatter.

"Not bad as armor goes," muses Amscusat. It is the standard armor for the great vessels. Pressure driven or magnetic trains connect all the under-armor points in a few minutes, driving around the great wells, where the fighter-ships and the ships for deep space and planetary density actions are located.

The 60,000 spaceships are kept inside one hundred-twenty "cartridges", each hosting five hundred. The ships are one on top of the other, in a sort of fast elevator, capable of shooting them out, at an average of twenty-five per second.

It is time to take a break. The visitors go straight down to the restoration level, where they are offered fresh cud, bones, candied fruit, rare meat just made in the lab: it is customary to offer well-wishing sweets to the guests, and anything that produces a pleasant relaxation, according to the tastes of each species.

The visitors exchange their impressions, ask all kinds of questions, according to their logic and species inclinations.

The most original observations are recorded, because good ideas often come from non-specialized people, and they give rise to new fanciful applications. At the agreed and chosen time, the visitors go to the spaces reserved for regeneration and sleep.

73

GENERALS MUST HAVE
A VIVID IMAGINATION

Affter a good sleep, Amscusat seeks out his friends. They eat together, and then they are ready to carry on with the guided visit. Today, they start with the small assault craft, whose docks they saw the day before.

These vessels have a diameter of about fifty meters, are eighteen meters high and host twenty fast mini-ships, each eight meters long, four meters wide and two meters high.

75

These very fast missiles are multi-use flying cannons, capable of shooting freshly generated anti-matter grains, or piercing, burning, freezing rays and any other beams that the battle-officers might choose. They also carry four robots, for individual actions, such as demolishers, occupiers, sappers and whatever else may be required.

So, we have been able to assess a "first call" deployment of 60,000 ships in one minute and twenty seconds, plus 1,200,000 mini-ships with four robots, that is almost five million basic robots.

Quite good if we consider that in case of need, in the meantime, smaller docks churn out of this great hive ten million average depth spheroships.

Each one of them has approximately one third of the power and the weapons of the fighter-ships.

Arielvo can also split itself up, into twenty-four sectors, that can each take on a drop-shape, suitable also for atmospheric penetration.

The visit goes on for days and days, here I am summing up the things that most interested Amscusat, up to his return to the mainland. I'll tell you, for instance, of the factories producing any object you can think of. Upon request, they can make any object, in a few seconds or in a maximum of a few minutes, starting from amorphous matter.

The generals who lead the ship must, more than anything else, have a vivid imagination. The Enemy, carrier of power, totally lacks this quality. I cannot describe the secret bridges, the truly creative weapons and the surprises already prepared for the next clashes!

Amscusat is also very curious about the whisk-cabins. They are as big as fighter-ships, made especially to project some of them at a great distance, from zero to the speed of light, in order to outflank pluridimensional positions.

There are whisks suitable for all kinds of transmission and reception, up to the distance of two light-days, if necessary. When these means cannot be used, it is the usual ships that intervene, for hand-to-hand fighting. They can disembark soldiers of any kind according to their assigned mission.

There are soldiers of the Tujlne races—the same as Necatoa, Amscusat's friend—and fighters belonging to species that Amscusat has never seen, and maybe never even heard of, so vast is the federation of the Living Worlds!

Toward the end of the visit, Amscusat finds out that this is a D-class ship, and there are up to M-class. Those are really great ships! A week would not even be enough to explore just one level of a vessel like those.

IN THIRDLIFE YOU FACE
THE ENEMY OF HUMANKIND

After these intense days on Arielvo, Amscusat gets back home. A nice surprise awaits him. The right amount of time has gone by, and his mother Mana is getting ready to give birth to her new child.

Mom has chosen a biological pregnancy and birth, instead of a more classic maturation of the fetus in a mechanical uterus. It will be a girl and her name will be Melte. She will develop considerable talents; she will surely be a wonderful sister.

Giving birth is a familiar thing. Amscusat does not have to wait long before father Codaji comes out of the room chosen for the delivery, holding his new baby daughter. He introduces her to Ilna and Amscusat.

Mom is well, everything went smoothly and joyfully. All the co-parents celebrate the event. Their friends bring gifts and it is a beautiful party.

A few days later, the little girl is perfectly integrated into her new life. Her introduction to the Temple of Lives has been made, the bonds tied, the tests to verify that there is no Enemy in her, carried out. Nowadays, the insertion into Life, at all levels, is carried out with great care.

79

Already, in firstlife, choices are guided, the newly-born are dedicated to Forces, till they reach the age of mature decisions.

Amscusat is happy that he now has a little sister. Her tender and defenseless presence reminds him of how beautiful life is, after the intense emotions he lived on Arielvo.

Enough with weapons now, and with the war he will have to face, too, in thirdlife. Enough with force that, unfortunately, we are obliged to use to combat the Enemy of Humankind. All civilized forms know how things are, which terrible dangers threaten the interracial civilization of the living worlds. Amscusat thinks of Arielvo's great temples, where the Gods arrange possible lines for the great galactic movements, through symmetries and applying impossible geometries. Only that category of life-form can do such things.

He thinks of the Grail chamber, where forces beyond imagination are present, which melt one with the other. He thinks of the pluridimensional container-fields, capable of geometrically containing a whole planet in a non-space only a few meters large.

But the Enemy is even stronger. It has even more powerful means. For such a long time, it has dominated from inside, from the hearts of the living species, teaching pain, evil, every negative and uncontrolled thing. It seems impossible, now.

Yet, not everyone feels the same way about the proper way to deal with it and within the galactic civilization there are two large political parties.

One maintains the need of a total destruction of the Enemy while the other—to which Amscusat now belongs—thinks that it is possible to defeat it without annihilating it.

Also these forces, albeit anti-life forces, must have a place, a space for existing. Amscusat though, is still full of doubts. He will have to make his full choice once he is older and more mature, with more information and experience.

GRAVIFOOTBALL SPORTS NEWS

A mscusat comes out of the house on his gravicycle. After the long visit to the spaceship, he really feels like a long cycle ride. He rides towards its favorite spot, where we found him at the beginning of this story.

Along the road, among the meadows and the trees of the outer city, he finds a distributor of video-bulletins and he buys one, in order to keep up with the latest regional and space news.

Sure, it would be easier to receive the news via his cerebral cortex, but he loves to read...

There are reports of research and progress in contacting psycho-forms, able to take on the protoplasmic appearance of elves and cobolds, fairies and gnomes. There are images of the liberation of another planet, of the systems that the Enemy used to keep it enslaved, more or less the usual, terrible ones. Truly, the Enemy has no imagination.

There are videopages that he skips completely, in order to linger on the gravifootball sports news. His favorite team won. He's happy, because he'll talk and laugh about it with his friends.

Amscusat is a fan of this sport, in which three teams at a time play one against the others, inside a large suspended sphere. They have to score with a random-degravitation ball, and they cannot make alliances to play against just one team.

Each player has fixed positions to defend and marks two other players, one for each adversary team. The best players describe extraordinary figures with their bodies as they fly weightless, without gravity.

Amscusat also loves *metratura*, he's actually an amateur *metrator*. Metratura is a meditation-sport technique of a very high level. Participants must move inside a definite space using all their senses, with full presence.

They must be completely aware of everything happening around them, also at a very big distance; of all processes, including the automatic ones, going on inside their bodies; and the movements of all other participants.

Once this state of presence is attained, they start moving, *metrating* the field they are on, without losing concentration and awareness.

Interspecies metratura competition is particularly fascinating, because the use of different senses makes it necessary to consider complex and various factors in the perception and interpretation of reality.

The video-paper talks about the competition that started just before he left for Arielvo, and had not yet concluded. It is a high level psycho-competition, with representatives of many species.

The human representatives are not winning, but their ranking is quite good.

Amscusat also likes the inter-racial games, the ones such as humans vs. zebras, or dogs vs. horses. Sometimes, there are also games suitable for alien forms, or hurdle-races with allied species, as in the humans-dolphins-flyers competitions.

He likes being informed about sport, a form of positive confrontation which, if not taken to excess, can joyfully educate all living beings to live together, with mutual respect. Amusement unites, play teaches, imagination is unleashed, and bodies are nourished with new ideas.

Amscusat likes to practice many sports, and to be always active and fit. Some time ago, though, he went through a difficult period: he had no energy and felt tired all the time. Mother was very worried, but analyses revealed that the problem was just in one of his subtle bodies, which was particularly fatigued.

Amscusat underwent a tonic treatment, using balancing patterns and drawings as well as sound-music, as advised by his family doctor.

Sometimes, pseudobodies suffer from energy deficiencies and this often preludes an illness, which, although curable in the special whisks, has its origin in the condition of the subtle bodies themselves. It is much better to intervene immediately, maybe using specific micro-attractors, those nano-materic energetic supports that, through the aura, convey the right information to the body so that the organs can work in the best possible way.

During his growth, in the rites of passage from first to secondlife, Amscusat has often energized himself with solar rocks, or by observing or finger-walking with great attention special patterns for his mind; or by using selfic instrumentation with special spirals.

At school, he often studies the principles of Selfica - the discipline that directs intelligent and specialized energies through supports made of metal or specific inks and liquids, and the science of the spirals of energy.

During his course of study in stable evocation, he already learnt, many years ago, how to summon up his energy-companion, an entity that can acquire consistency, thanks to the usual magic practices, and can even manifest itself independently, in case of need.

In secondlife, he will learn how to call up his future Spirit Guide, that soul guardian everyone has, the ultimate defense in case of mortal Enemy attack.

NEW FORMS CAPABLE
OF HOSTING A SOUL

A mscusat has finally arrived at his beloved place where, some time before, he became friends with a dolphin, called Melnun. It called him a few hours ago, asking to meet there.

While waiting for his friend, Amscusat keeps reading the other news on the daily video-paper. New treaties are being prepared, with species that are soon to join the vital alliance.

There is news on the habits of abyss creatures from a far planet, and about the markets and new products for sale. For example, a very beautiful type of under-shoe for water-skating, guaranteed for a greater depth than the ones he now uses. They would be just right for going to see Melnun.

His friend arrives soon, they meet in the water, and they greet each other with joy and fondness. The translator allows both of them to talk to each other, without any problems. The device translates their emotions, as well. Being good friends, both of them agree to set it onto the highest level. In this way there is no filter, and the emotional exchange is profound and complete.

The world must have been so sad when species were not talking to each other, when they knew nothing about each other's way of living, feeling and thinking!

The two friends look at the open seas, down there where many species do not have a common consciousness yet, where life is wild and pure, where life and death take turns in a natural and smooth way. There is the kingdom of the new forms, the primordial place for the maturation of distinctions, where the souls go from one existence to another, frenetically, ineluctably.

Richness is in variety, and today in the world, there are many species which were once extinct, and have been brought back to life through cloning and genetic reconstruction, in balance with modern forms that survived and evolved. A few years have already passed since a reconstructed species, a gregarious race of dinosaurs, has been admitted into the multivital alliance, because it was recognized as intelligent.

Other species, once extinct, are now about to be welcomed back among living beings. Even new forms– partly mechanical, partly biological–have been recognized as capable of hosting a soul, and also certain pure computers have got this characteristic.

Not everybody worries about death, but there are people who have a spare mechanical body, capable of containing their soul, in the event of a mortal accident. This extraordinary possibility has been arranged also for people who are essential for this epoch, even though it is a sacrifice for them, because it binds them to this time.

In this period of war against the Enemy, we cannot allow too much time to pass, for these key people, between one reincarnation and the next. These are the beings that are leading the battle and carry out important tasks for the survival of all the species.

Their continuous presence in command must be guaranteed. Immediate reincarnation is one of the most efficient systems at the moment. Therefore, there are places, specifically set up for this procedure, with special bodies ready to be used.

Amscusat once visited one such place, and from the Temple linked to it he communicated with the paradivine forms responsible for that task. This event touched him very deeply, leaving an ineffable sensation in him.

It is, at the same time, relaxing and stimulating to chat with Melnun. Their mutual curiosity, their reciprocal esteem, the stories about the things they consider important, are fundamental elements in a supra-racial society.

Who knows what the world was like when knowledge was limited, when species were killing each other or, even worse, when they were dominated by one race or the other, with great cruelty!

After their meeting, it is time for the two of them to get back home.

ORONAAVO'S CELEBRATION

A t home, Amscusat tells his parents about the people he met, what he felt and lived, his most interesting thoughts. The sun Lavallaorò, as always, darts fast in the sky.

Oromè slowly follows it, or is overtaken. Tonight, the moons are going to be simultaneously visible in the sky. The night will become very bright, while the yearly comet looks larger, during its usual approach to the planet.

In the whole larger region, this will be a celebration night, a very old celebration, which occurs twice a year, with the warm weather and in the coldest season. For weeks, the trees have been preparing for this ritual moment, during which all the living worlds will be in contact with each other, and the natural roads of the Synchronic Lines open up.

The celebration of Oronaavo is the most important, the one which allows the souls to transit to the worlds where their new reincarnation will occur. So, it is essential that everybody participates in the rituals, opening and guaranteeing these possibilities, which the Enemy hid and forbade in the past.

91

All the bridge-species - those connecting the material plane with the divine one - are involved in this important cosmic appointment with renewal. Many ninthlifers choose this moment to leave their body, after careful counseling with the Gods and with the appropriate forces.

This is also the occasion to determine the number of births that will occur in the year, considering the reincarnated people about to leave and to arrive, and the members of species going towards the higher experience levels of other species, up to the bridge-species.

The celebration requires large circles, traced on the ground in the old fashion, and charged with well balanced psychic energy and power-will. It is also harvest-time for the substance-non-substance, useful for the magical practices of the year.

This special subtle element develops on the land near the Synchronic Lines, especially where the living species are in balance, and the thoughts and behaviors of the beings that live there are pure and lofty, rich in vision and complexity of love.

At the moment of the great Ritual, everybody stands in a circle, holding each other's hands or in physical contact, all humans together, and the animals divided by species.

In the sea, the water species perform their rituals in the proper way, as the whole plantity quivers, getting ready to project the prepared souls far away, and to receive the ones that are traveling, through a synchronic temporal adjustment.

Certain human worlds call these moments Solstices. They are the great rituals of union among species and races, when living forms recognize themselves as deriving from one single matrix.

EXCHANGE OF BODY WITH THE FALNEMANJ BERALCO

T ime goes by. Amscusat lives his usual life. He grows up and prepares himself to become a thirdlifer, in some years. His potentialities are developing, his co-parents and parents look after him carefully; he has many friends and becomes more and more aware of the direction of his life.

Now, he is preparing for an exchange of body with a Falnemanj. He will "lend" his body and will receive and use, in exchange, that of his correspondent on the far away planet, where it lives. It is easy to understand why his parents hesitate: the guest will use Amscusat's body and, as it is not be used to it, they will have to take care of it all the time. A special computer will lead it, throughout its stay, and Amscusat's body will wear special clothes, manifesting its condition of willing possession.

The Falnemanj's name is Beralco. It lives in a rather far system and its race is similar to birds. Yet, they cannot fly; they run and jump from one large platform to another, structures similar to very tall elastic mushrooms.

Gravity, on the world it lives in, is slightly stronger than on Amscusat's planet.

95

It is a world with few seas and with immense plains, covered by this particular kind of tree-platform, eighty meters tall on average, on top of which the Falnemanj race lives.

Their jumps are a very normal way of moving around for them, but very difficult for a human. Likewise, walking on the ground will be contrary to Beralco's nature.

These are only a few of the difficulties that they will have to face in exchanging their bodies. For instance, they'll have to adapt and feed themselves with foods suitable for their body and not for their mind and the sense of taste they are accustomed to, in the body they normally use on their worlds of origin.

For some weeks, on their own planets, Amscusat and Beralco have trained for this exchange and they have learned what was necessary to adapt to each other, without risking the creation of excessive damage to their respective hosting bodies.

Automatic physiological processes such as sleep, defecation, intake of food and liquids will have to be respected with extreme care. Moreover, it will be difficult to breathe, because the Falnemanjs use special under-wing pores, from where, through internal body decompression, the special gas mixture they need enters their body. It is as if they breathed by moving their arms, while for humans it is a whole different story.

For Amscusat, the preparation for the experience is therefore long and complex, carefully guided by his personal computer, which will be modified for the new situation, the new language, the arrival position he will have to keep in order to enter Beralco's body in the appropriate way and take over its control immediately.

The contacts between Amscusat's species and that of his next guest are not ancient, indeed they are quite recent. There are still many things to be found out from one another.

Therefore, Beralco trains in the same scrupulous way on its own planet: everybody wants these exchanges to happen in a safe and pleasant way, as they are so important to get to know different ways of being and thinking.

Amscusat also visits multi-species friends and acquaintances which have already had experiences inside exchanged bodies, and they always talk about them as very important events, which increases their prestige among friends.

97

Often, experiences in different bodies are carried out on the same planet, inside the bodies of dolphins, horses, dogs, whales, sentient birds, and dozens and dozens of other races, linked by the Interspecies Treaty. Exchanges with friends from other worlds are a bit rarer.

Amscusat is happy about it. He's proud, but also a bit scared, because of the strange behavior that Beralco will certainly have in the first experiences inside his body.

He's mostly afraid of making a fool of himself, and he worries that friends will jokingly laugh at him... He also knows that this is not regarded as a very evolved way of thinking, but he justifies himself by saying that, after all, he's just a second-life boy.

He must also think about what he himself will do inside Beralco's body. He will have to pay attention, a lot of attention, in order not to cause any damage. But, all in all, he knows that everything will go well, thanks to their thorough preparation.

A FIRSTWORLD PRISON
FOR GODS

O ne day, when Oromè is high and Lavallaorò is soaring fast, Amscusat has the opportunity, according to his program of studies, to visit the Center for the Liberation of Worlds. It is there that the Envoys-to-be are prepared to join in the dominating race-type on the various planets, together with the objects used for their rescue missions.

99

To civilizations that are still slaves of the Enemy–those which have developed systems of writing based on sight, scents, chemical signals or carved with sound–special texts are sent, magic or reference scripts, suitable for the ways of thinking of those living species.

These scripts are prepared to contain formulae of power, with which to infiltrate the Enemy's ranks, and little by little, dissolve the chains of evil. It is an awe-inspiring, very important task.

Many sacred texts speak of the end times of each planet, when the Forces of union will triumph and the species will be for ever freed and re-united in justice. There are also many Gods who accept to go for very long periods of time to those important worlds, in those key places.

Sometimes, even the Gods were imprisoned by the Enemy forces and kept for millennia in a sleeping state or with reduced powers. There is even a fundamental world, a firstworld, where there is a sort of prison for Gods, where many powerful Divine Lords are detained and time-bound.

The dream of every secondlifer, and not theirs alone, is to one day be able to free that world and break off the evil power by means of the divine revolt. Many sacred texts write about the end of times of every planet, when the forces of the union will triumph, and when the species will be totally freed and reunited in justice.

Many books are sent, through the dreams of special residents of those planets. Others are handed down orally.

Suitable magic practices and fundamental teachings are widely spread orally allowing, little by little, the opening of the inner room of the soul for every species. Many races do not even know what it is, they have no idea of their divine nature, agitating in their silent souls.

Many worlds are backward and enslaved. They are overtaken by bestiality and enormously reduced in their natural powers, in their goodness, and in their universal love.

But one day, Amscusat thinks, he will also go on those worlds, to do his task. He will then act like a hero, he will bring forth some changes on those cosmic islands. He will fight for knowledge and for the reunification of the human species.

Sometimes, Amscusat is in a hurry to grow up, to trace back his previous existences and to reconnect with his latest task, that of of his present life. He throbs with energy and enthusiasm; this is the subject they often talk about among friends.

School, visits and their many tasks: the purpose of all of them is to prepare the new generations for the ultimate fight, for achieving the very goal of the present civilization.

All beings must be freed, all forms hosting human souls, in every world, in every epoch, in every motherworld of the perceptible universe, at every thinkable level and dimension.

Universal evolution demands it, for life and against anti-life, the absolute death that the Enemy wants. Study, study.

THE VARIOUS KINDS
OF TIME TRAVEL

S tarting from fourthlife, there are envoys being trained or already fully operative. There have magic instruments they can use, according to the laws of every cluster of worlds.

They are sent holding in their memory (whether bio or mec) the construction steps of magic devices, so that they can fully use special powers for their just as special goals. Sometimes, on some planets, specific agents leave devices and tools behind, so that other beings like them will be able to recognize them and use them in later time fractions.

At the moment, on Amscusat's planet, many kinds of time travel are practized, among which the main ones are as follows:

- informative, through out-of-body channels;
- exploratory, through experiences inside animals, entered without them knowing;
- entering human bodies at birth;
- through direct biological sending;
- through telepathic and séance contact;
- through time-radio signals;

103

- through divinatory communication;
- through signals left from the future or from the past; through gravitational pressure;
- through succession from echo or parallel worlds, or time branches at the end of a time packet;
- through divine intercession or Grail intervention.

If we consider also the use of magic instruments and special Cabins as well as the natural predisposition of such races such as the Setjpeals, which can send back into the past, for a few seconds at a time, the predators attacking them, we can say that time is abundantly crossed far and wide, as the fishes cross the sea.

Other normal systems of time travel are psychometry, history and memory, and life. For example, the large rivers of time, such as the future, are navigated in a natural way by all the species of this small piece of time-space, which hosts you reader NOW. (*And this is a typical consideration of a time diary, like the one assigned to/ chosen by Amscusat when he plays by himself, sending himself messages at a distance, from the future to the past, as he's doing NOW.*)

During his out-of-body journey courses, Amscusat has learned how to enter magic libraries, at various levels of penetration. These are the places where in every important world, essential knowledge for the species that live on that world is contained.

They hold also the known and shared archetypes, as well as the security systems to recognize the ones which have been subtracted from the species subjected to the Enemy's control.

Occupations and liberations, followed again by new Enemy invasions, led to the setting up, through time, of these safety deposits of knowledge. Parallel to this, some individuals with a fighter instinct have been prepared, men and women capable of using "natural" qualities which are normally seen as superior.

Also the other species, each one in its own way, have developed beings with special powers, for all eventualities. The biggest trouble arises when one of the bridge-species belonging to a key world loses Consciousness up to the point that it destroys other species, even leading to their complete extinction.

Also Netila, who is very thrilled about time travel, would like someday to become a traveler-assistant, on some natural world to be freed and saved.

She has already tried it in other lives. Maybe someday, her dream will come true, unless the Enemy is defeated and sent away before then.

Amscusat thinks of his own family and of all the things already done by the adults. And absurdly enough, he wonders if there will be something left also for him to do...

SOUL DIALOGUE
BETWEEN TREES
AND HUMANS

F or example, Ilna, Amscusat's genetic brother, is interested in trees and since he is a thirdlifer, he has more and more important roles, as he matures.

He carried out a mission as an incognito civil instructor, among the humanoid population of a planet at a second level of civilization. This thrilled him, and now, he talks to everybody about it as he would like to continue working in this field.

Establishing contact with alien people is not easy. Often, it is necessary to communicate first with other base-forms, or bridge-forms, of that world, and then to create the suitable time condition and eventually, according to the thought-forms of the chosen species, take on the adequate body or form.

As for usage and custom of the language, there are often no recordings extant, to base one's talk on, so it is necessary to improvise and look as native as possible. Often enough, the pseudobodies prepared in special ships are sufficient to blend in with the beings chosen for contact, but it is then necessary to learn to change form, according to time, to the possible need of aging, or to changes in circumstances and habits.

In the world where Ilna went, trees are closely connected to the life of the dominant form. They have been adapted as homes, and are carefully taken care of, in a truly symbiotic way.

Once chosen, the tree is never left, for a whole life. For very special events, or in case of necessary transferals of their symbiont, the trees are transported and then re-planted in the chosen place. If a tree dies, the being that inhabited it unfailingly dies, too. In the same way, young trees dies if something irreparable befalls the humanoid of which they are the symbiont.

The soul dialogue among these two species is very intense, consistent and continuous. Sometime, plants and humans happen to argue, and they start to play endless tricks on each other: inner pod-doors drying up, leaves that no longer shield from the sun, and in return, less care to the roots and reduced fertilizers...

In some cases, there is an actual divorce between humanoid and plant, and everyone talks about it, with much grieving and scandal. A local proverb says that it is much better to lose a relative than to argue with one's tree. And all this, Ilna maintained, was really true.

For Ilna himself, the major difficulty was finding a suitable tree, an original kind of plant, with innovative political ideas, open enough to accept what he secretly represented for that world. Eventually he found one, a divorced tree that didn't want to deal anymore with know-all tripeds.

Yes, the inhabitants of that planet are tripeds, with three prehensile feet, a short tail for communicating by shaking it against the drum-leaves, and two scarcely developed upper limbs, similar to arms with four-fingered hands.

Amscusat had a lot of fun, looking at images of his brother inside that body, they exchanged fast and cutting jokes, but always pleasant.

After an intense day, after losing himself thousands and thousands times in thoughts and anxieties, typical of his age, Amscusat decides to properly prepare himself for the exchange with Beralco, and he starts studying, with great focus, all the implications of his next adventure.

EXPERIENTIAL PERFUMES TEACH THE MIND

O nly a few days to the body exchange. So many things to do. Amscusat promised to get a bit further in his studies and in the normal work tasks of his age. On his world, everybody works throughout their life, the young and the less young. Working is a philosophy, a pleasure, a duty, a vital necessity.

Amscusat deals in experiential perfumes, those which, when sniffed, teach the mind many different things. The perfumes are carried around in small containers, the diffusers acting through the skin, by contact and through the sense of smell. They are typical of other species, but some time ago they were adapted for humans, as well. Information, history, planetary geography, and especially emotional news, can be taught this way. Olfactory poetry is very much in demand.

Amscusat is a salesman and also takes part in the making of some easily made kinds of perfumes. To this aim he often meets up with a fifthlifer, called Fasetdottijal, an original poet and a man of vital and sparkling temper. Poetry is very important in the world. It is used to communicate between the species, and it is also a great weapon against the Enemy.

For certain types of planetary ship, the poetry-ships, the main task is to launch on worlds, still occupied by the Enemy or its allies, poetry-perfumes suitable for living forms in slavery. Where reading exists, they diffuse scripts and poetry books, to obstruct and contrast the action of the anti-life principle and free the living from the destroyer Enemy.

Also, some kinds of music have the same aim. Others kinds are used by the Enemy itself to do the opposite. There have been planets the Enemy occupied by Evil by diffusing music in a particular way, or through forms of depression and pessimism. Other worlds have been freed using the same base-system plus poetry, singing, philosophy, motivations for living and respect for different species.

The most dangerous Enemy viruses are envy, using false words, negative thought, violence, denigrating the value of what others do and all the possible excesses of jealousy, rage and falsehood. Nowadays, the study of all excesses led by alien and negative forces, is a curriculum subject in every school, and in all individual or family study programs.

The philosophical bases that the Enemy forces have used for thousands of years are analyzed, together with the actions that have made so many species slaves one to the other, making them unhappy, and consequently furnishing plenty of nullifying and anti-life power to the Enemy. Many things are considered as diseases, and fought as such, with the correct means.

ONLY ONE HAPPY PARADISE

I n the great centers of research-contact among living species, relations with cloud-forms of a few worlds have been established and it has been discovered that on another world life is represented by a wind-species, composed of molecules in psycho-magnetic relation.

And in other planets live underground species, made of rocks and melted metals, at incommensurable pressures. Others still, host living waters. To sum up, sentient life can be recognized in any kind of form. There are fortunate worlds, where everything is alive: waters, air, earth, fire-creatures, which nourish themselves with dry vegetables, or eat melted rocks or natural gases.

There is neutrinic life inside the burning suns. For them, our matter has no density. It is as thought is to us. Such a hyper-dense species are they that for them planets are simply hypothetical. They only exists as infinitesimal fields of quasi-matter. Suns are almost cold for them; solar wind is their normal route for going from one star to another.

Yet our life species have contacted these forms, using superdense neutrino signals and taking thousands of years as the flowing of time for these forms is computed differently.

These are forms that can otherwise be contacted only by the right Gods. A thousand years for them is less than a minute for us.

There is sentient life among stars, species that, opposite to the superdense neutrino species, are super-rarefied, and whose minimum extension reaches a half light-year.

One day, not too far away, maybe, the galactic civilization will include all living forms, of every category, of every level and dimension. The bridge-forms will then be able to fully accomplish their ultimate goal, and be the fundamental fabric for the recomposition and the awareness of extreme unity, infinity of conscience, without any boundaries between Gods and bacteria.

Every Primeval Divinity will eventually conceive the happy thought-form, a unity-consciousness, which can be traversed by individual lives, in the infinite and in the ultimate mystery, irreversibly, where the tiny self-consciousness of every particle will have nobility and certitudes. Every conception will be possible, everything will be feasible, only one happy paradise of awareness and knowledge, infinitely linked.

This is the courageous dream of the human-forms, of those divinely allied, in opposition to absolute disunity, the destruction pursued by the Enemy. If it were to win, there will be no more life, just pure pain, irreversible, indissoluble, consciously unremovable.

There will be no escape, nor beneficent and freeing death, only an infinite sea of pain, of rejections, of impossibilities and regrets—all things which nourish evil.

There will only be infinite defeats, immense alienations, to be individually borne.

The species will cause each other pain and suffering without hope, as they will be certain of the Enemy's omnipotence. There will be no resignation, because it will be made impossible; the abyss of evil will have infinite depth, will be unreachable, and everybody will be certain that salvation will never arrive, in any way, from anywhere, ever.

This is the war the species are fighting. Now we are winning. And the Enemy is being banished from millions of worlds, faster and faster, as civilization is finally making its first steps. We hope that no evil virus has remained behind, hidden somewhere, ready to hit again and make us lose the victories we have already accomplished.

This very clash between the two different political theses—the one that chooses to simply send away the evil forces and confine them in a safe place; and the other which, on the contrary, wants to wipe it out completely—will be decisive.

Amscusat and his family are in favor of the first thesis, others in favor of the second. Everybody hopes that, whatever happens, there will be no mistake and the choice, soon to be made by universal vote, will be the right one. On the one hand, some people think that total annihilation would be applying the Enemy's own method, an anti-life choice.

On the other, the idea is, that if we do not destroy it completely, the Enemy might one day deceitfully make a return, and take the living species back into the abysm, turning one against the other, and making them lose knowledge and awareness.

The Gods will abstain from voting, because the choice is limited to the species that live inside of matter, the realm invaded by the Enemy, within time.

FROM THE TREE OF AWARENESS THE SPHERE WAS PICKED

We know how this story ended. The confinement party won, and a few thousand years later, the Enemy deceitfully attacked again, bringing with it, division and disunion, creating little by little, a racist movement, once more skilfully diffusing its viruses.

Species became disunited. They were again led to conceive fight and engage in it, because they had forgotten the use of weapons and the very idea of struggle. Many Gods abandoned the species that were losing awareness despite their many warnings.

Preparations for a future war started. Strongholds were secretly established on the key worlds, to rise again, without ever forgetting that the first answer was wrong. So, in that time, from the Tree of Awareness, the sphere was picked; the unity to long for; the outline of the path and the memory, especially of what had happened and what the Enemy - as winner of the battle - had taken away from humankind and from Lives.

A new, long path was ahead of the living species. Alliances were to be made again.

117

Memories were to be brought back. The Envoy-agents started to take action again. What had been dissolved, was to be bound again. It was necessary to guide the steps of a once-more blind humanity, acting a little by little to react against the reigning evil.

Secret plans, prepared in very ancient times, began to be enacted. The secret weapons were found again. The Gods were awakened and united. Planets were freed. The old covenants were claimed. And answers were requested, for those promises humanity itself had long forgotten.

Secret agents, during past human events, used powerful means, prepared in those times when victory was near, but few had really understood just how close-by the danger was.

The paths of pain were walked on. Evil and desperation were tasted, in all their possible flavors, so that we would not forget again. Little by little, humanity searched for its own path, among unspeakable errors and horrors, building history.

The powers clashed again. Secret points started to be active, waiting for the final Envoys. Messiahs came. Lives were heroically donated, and spent, for a higher goal. The planes of reality and time were separated and ancient Forces came into play, Forces that had been kept as the one last chance.

Ancient companions of oaths, at the limits of time, were called back. Powerful knights who had forgotten everything, lost because of the Enemy.

The time of the final battles had come. Secret weapons were to be carefully prepared. Magical forces were fully reawakened.

The very ancient ship Arielvo, traveler of skies, is still hidden. She is the last survivor of an immense fleet, but for a thousand millennia she has been building inside her bowels the weapons necessary for resurrection. She has the accumulated abilities of one thousands worlds, the knowledge of millions of years.

She still knows how to send souls to the worlds she is helping to free, and then call them back again. The Gods living in her know how to invite humankind to freedom. From her secret dimension, she watches over the efforts of the little humans.

Assamen the Old is still alive, at a standstill. Sleepy, but ready to lead the new-found forces, against an omnipresent Enemy. The anti-viruses against those of the Enemy–distributed through respected formulas and oaths and ritually made effective–are active and make the chosen men and women worthy of their nobility and their word.

There are relapses into evil, but they are diseases which can be overcome by the ancient power contained in those who, partly re-awakened, have been called to the new era, to the battle, to the war of liberation of humankind. With strength and patience, with courage and awareness, if free will is firmly directed, it leads to salvation - it is possible.

February 21st 1992, 21/16/XVII

DAMANHUR, FEDERATION OF COMMUNITIES

Damanhur is a Federation of Spiritual Communities in Italy founded in 1974. The first group came to live in Baldissero Canavese, in the province of Turin, in 1979, and has since grown to 25 communities. With just under a thousand people connected to the project, some reside in the communities and others participate more autonomously in research and meditation activities around the world. Damanhur recognizes citizenship to those living in the federation, as well as those who live and support its shared spiritual ideals even while not living in a community. Damanhurians adopt animal and plant names as a symbol of personal renewal through a connection with nature.

Falco Tarassaco, née Oberto Airaudi (philosopher, mystic, healer, writer and painter, 1950 - 2013), was the founder and spiritual leader of Damanhur.

The spiritual philosophy researches contact with the divine matrix of the universe through self-reflection, relations with others, encounters with nature and the study of esoteric traditions of various cultures and peoples. The Damanhurian centers in Italy and in other countries are places of cultural activity and spiritual research, as well as laboratories for artisan works, transformation of food, and much more. The path to spiritual growth encourages the application in daily life—in every expression of human life—of ethical principles characterized by solidarity and sustainability, which can be seen in the many activities in Damanhurian communities and centers.

Damanhurians believe that a spiritual project needs a well-defined organizational structure. For this reason, Damanhur has a written Constitution and the social system includes elected roles, meeting procedures and decisions based on shared rules.

The Federation is an articulated, democratic, highly participatory society active in local politics—presenting electoral lists and engaged in the administration of some local governments. It uses a complementary currency called the "Credito" (credit)—of equal value to the euro—which is even accepted by some local businesses that are not part of Damanhur.

Art in all forms and expressions (music, theater, painting, sculpture...) is considered a tool of self-knowledge and actualization—a way to give voice to the experiences and feelings of all the Damanhurian popolo (population/people).

The Temples of Humankind is the meeting point between art and spirituality. The most well-known work of art at Damanhur, it is a complex of halls and corridors dug by hand (300,175 ft3) completely underground. After digging and building walls, ceilings and floors, Damanhurians have richly decorated each space with mosaics, paintings, glass art and cupulas. The Temples are dedicated to Beauty and Harmony as instruments for the ascension of humanity.

The Federation of Communities invests heavily in hospitality and in welcoming guests to come visit. It is also involved in various academic and university-level research studies.

Damanhur is a member of GEN Europe (Global Ecovillage Network) and RIVE (Rete Italiana Villaggi Ecologici; Italian Network of Ecovillages), who collect the community and eco-living experiences in Italy and beyond, and of CONACREIS (Coordinamento Nazionale Associazioni e Comunità di Ricerca Etica Interiore Spirituale; National Coordination of Associations and Community that Research Ethical Inner Spirituality).

It is possible to get to know Damanhur online, from bookstores, in conferences and courses offered by Damanhurians, and of course, by visiting the Federation in person for a few days or longer.

Damanhur, Federation of Communities
10080 Baldissero C.se (TO) - Italy
www.damanhur.org

www.ingramcontent.com/pod-product-compliance
Lightning Source LLC
Chambersburg PA
CBHW072357190626
46811CB00019B/1209